Busy Babies
Go to the Gym

Written by Jane Kemp and Clare Walters

Illustrated by Alex Ayliffe

Collins

An imprint of HarperCollinsPublishers

Come on, Mum!

Sharing Books From Birth to Five

Welcome to Practical Parenting Books

It's never too early to introduce a child to books. It's wonderful to see your baby gazing intently at a cloth book; your toddler poring over a favourite picture; or your older child listening quietly to a story. And you're his favourite storyteller, so have fun together while you're reading – use silly voices, linger over the pictures and leave pauses for your child to join in.

In *Busy Babies Go To The Gym* your baby will see other babies just like him climbing on the big play equipment. Sing the nursery rhymes, emphasise the sounds like 'Wheee' and 'Bump' and talk to your baby about the lively activities. Perhaps even finish with a scramble over some cushions on your living room floor!

Books open doors to other worlds, so take a few minutes out of your busy day to cuddle up close and lose yourselves in a story. Your child will love it – and so will you.

Jane & Clare

Jane Kemp   Clare Walters

P.S. Look out, too, for *Busy Babies Go Swimming*, the companion book in this age range, and all the other great books in the new Practical Parenting series.

AGE
1-2

First published in Great Britain by HarperCollins*Publishers* Ltd in 2000

1 3 5 7 9 8 6 4 2

ISBN: 0-00-136137-6

The Practical Parenting/HarperCollins pre-school book series has been created by Jane Kemp and Clare Walters.
The Practical Parenting imprimatur is used with permission by IPC Magazines Ltd.

Practical Parenting is published monthly by IPC Magazines Ltd.
For subscription enquiries and orders, ring 01444 445555
or the credit card hotline (UK orders only) on 01622 778778.

The HarperCollins website address is: www.**fire**and**water**.com

Printed and bound in Hong Kong.

Busy babies want to go to the gym.

Click, click! Quick, let's find Rosie.

Look, there's Sam.

We want to play!

Bounce!

Slide!

Let's do... everything!

HORSEY, HORSEY, DON'T YOU STOP,
JUST LET YOUR FEET GO CLIPETTY CLOP.
YOUR TAIL GOES SWISH AND THE WHEELS GO ROUND,
GIDDY UP, WE'RE HOMEWARD BOUND!

Hold on tight, we're off for a ride.

One, two, three, wheeeeeeeee!

Bump!

First me. Whoosh! Now you!

TWO YOUNG GENTLEMEN MET IN A LANE,
BOWED MOST POLITELY, BOWED ONCE AGAIN.
HOW DO YOU DO, AND HOW DO YOU DO?
AND HOW DO YOU DO AGAIN!

One step, two step... wibble-wobble.

Shiffle-shuffle. Shiffle-shuffle.

Peep-po! Here I am!

Busy babies need their naps now.

Sharing Books From Birth to Five

£3.99

0 00 136130 9

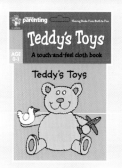

£3.99

0 00 136132 5

£3.99

0 00 136139 2

£3.99

0 00 136137 6

AGE 0–1

AGE 1–2

£3.99

0 00 136147 3

£3.99

0 00 136171 6

£3.99

0 00 136151 1

£3.99

0 00 136153 8

AGE 2–3

AGE 3–5

The Practical Parenting books are available from all good bookshops and can be ordered direct from HarperCollins Publishers by ringing 0141 7723200 and through the HarperCollins website: www.**fire**and**water**.com

You can also order any of these titles, with free post and packaging, from the Practical Parenting Bookshop on 01326 569339 or send your cheque or postal order together with your name and address to: Practical Parenting Bookshop, Freepost, PO Box 11, Falmouth, TR10 9EN.